I Should Have Told You

By

Joanne Clancy

Joanne Clancy

ISBN-13:
978-1506180922

ISBN-10:
1506180922

Prologue

October 25th, 1969

The infant's hungry cries pierced the night air. Infuriated, his father threw the duvet aside and leapt out of bed. He hurried to the chest of drawers that doubled as the baby's cot. Angrily, he slammed the drawer closed. Inside, the wails soon turned to gasps as the baby struggled for air...

Joanne Clancy

Part 1

2013

Chapter 1

The killer cruised the empty, moonlit streets lined with naked trees, Georgian terraces, and high-rise flats that towered into the black sky. He pulled his tweed cap low over his eyes and scanned the streets.

There was no sign of her. He'd passed a few women standing on the street corners, but they weren't the one he wanted. He'd know her as soon as he laid eyes on her.

The killer was a lean man, average height. He wore a black wool coat and brown corduroy trousers. A hammer lay on the back seat.

A young blonde woman got out of her car and hurried up the steps to her house. She glanced uncertainly over her shoulder before opening the front door and switching on the hall lights. She lingered on the threshold for a minute, sensing someone out there, watching and waiting. Shivering, she locked the door carefully behind her.

The killer stared at the house. Lights came on upstairs. The woman came to the bedroom window and looked down the street, peering into the blackness. Then she drew the curtains tight and switched off the light.

The killer continued driving. Then he saw her, staggering slightly. She stuck out a hand to flag him down. The street was deserted. His hands started to tremble on the steering wheel. The uncontrollable force empowered and transformed him. He rolled down his window. "Need a lift, love?"

She'd do nicely…

Chapter 2

It was a dangerous proposition: sex for money with a complete stranger. Cold, scared, and alone: just where the killer wanted her. She had smiled her most beguiling smile at the driver who had picked her up, and now she was dead. The fog that clung grimly to her frail corpse as she lay on the edge of the riverbank shrouded her body.

Exactly thirty-two minutes after the body of Linda Keenan was found, the telephone rang beside Detective Chief Inspector George Ellis' bed. Early morning calls were nothing new for the head of Dublin's Crimes Against The Person Unit.

Bleary-eyed, he squinted against the darkness to check the time. It was 7.02a.m. He had finally dozed off an hour earlier. He grabbed the phone. "Ellis," he barked.

"There's been a murder, sir," the desk sergeant advised. "A jogger discovered a woman's body at Stephen's Green. Officers are at the scene."

"I'm on my way." He struggled out of bed.

Gina was already in the kitchen, making coffee. She knew what to expect. There was no point in cooking him breakfast. He'd have a quick shower, dress, and grab an apple on his way out the door. It would be midnight before she saw him again.

"There's been a murder," he explained, already shrugging into his heavy overcoat. He took a quick gulp of his coffee and kissed her goodbye.

"Take care," she said, and then he was gone. She watched through the living-room window as he reversed his decayed old Ford Escort down the drive and onto the road. For the hundredth time, she wondered if she'd ever see him again.

***

A freelance journalist arrived at the park before George. The crime scene investigators had not yet put up a screen to protect the body from inquisitive eyes. Standing at a safe distance, the journalist looked through the viewfinder of his camera, where he could clearly see the body of a woman lying on her back one hundred metres away.

Two police officers dragging a tarpaulin screen towards the woman distorted his view. Then the crime scene photographer moved into frame, his camera already clamped to a tripod. The journalist had only moments to take the shot before the image was obscured completely.

News crews and journalists quickly arrived, anxious to obtain a statement from DCI George Ellis. A buzz went around when they saw his hulking figure walk across the green, his broad shoulders hunched into his heavy black overcoat.

The journalists needed the goodwill of the man in charge. Likewise, George knew he would need help from the public to solve the murder. The news crews were a valuable resource, and as much as he disliked them, he'd ensure they'd have their story in time for the morning editions. He nodded at them as he made his way towards his colleagues.

It was cold and damp and the low-lying fog was doing nothing to improve his mood. The officers stamped their feet and folded their arms tight in an effort to keep warm. Some of them had been at the scene for over an hour. It was mid-November and winter had already set in.

Officers had put down a series of boards across the muddy area by the riverbank. George walked carefully on the slatted wood. The victim lay on her back. Her handbag was beside her. Her blue jeans had been pulled down below her knees and her top had been ripped open to expose her breasts.

Blood from stab wounds had dried on her body. Her dark, curly hair was spread out on the grass behind her head. She was still wearing underwear. A few coins were scattered in the nearby grass and a button lay beside her left hand. She had a stab wound to her throat, several to her breasts and a series of stab wounds across her stomach.

By the time the Coroner's Officer, Sharon Tierney, arrived an hour later George knew the dead woman's name and the fact that she had lived only a few hundred metres away. The terrace where she lived was across the road from the green.

Officers making house-to-house inquiries learned that Linda Keenan lived with her three young children and had recently divorced her husband. The eldest child went searching for her mother at first light when she woke up and found she hadn't been home all night.

Ten-year-old Aisling went to wait at the nearby bus stop for her mother. She was standing there, shivering, when a neighbor found her wearing her school coat over her pyjamas.

The house, when police searched it, was dirty and there was little food in the cupboards or fridge. Nothing surprised George anymore; he'd seen it all. Desperate women. Hungry children. Social workers had already been contacted about the children. No one knew where their father lived.

He wondered if her death was a domestic abuse incident that had gotten out of hand and that maybe her ex-husband was involved, until the neighbours told him that Linda often went out at night and was paid for her company. George sighed; the fact that she was a prostitute would complicate the investigation. Random prostitute murders were every investigator's worst nightmare. Experience had proven that the public was somehow not surprised at what happened to those women.

"Maybe we'll get lucky and solve the case quickly," Sharon said, clutching her coffee cup for warmth. She was blonde and lean, tense by nature, five feet ten, and hard-faced, but George respected her professionalism. She wore a forensic suit and plastic bootees over her shoes.

"Or maybe not," George shrugged.

"It's going to be another long day," she sighed.

George nodded, noticing the dark circles under her eyes. They had already spent most of the night together at another crime scene: a gangland murder on the other side of the city. Like George, she had only just dozed off to sleep when the call came through about the murdered woman. He filled her in on the details.

Sharon, notebook in hand, listened intently, as she always did. She looked around the body, drawing a quick diagram and taking notes.

"It looks like she was stabbed to death where she lay," she said, running her fingers through her short blonde hair. "See the way the blood-trickle runs into the top of her underwear and then along it."

Later, when the underwear was removed, she could see the trickle did not run down inside, suggesting that no intercourse had occurred immediately before or after the stabbing.

She took some swabs and then began measuring the temperature of the body. "From my quick calculations, I would say that death occurred around 1a.m.," she said as the body was gently wrapped in a large plastic sheet for the short journey to the morgue.

George and his team gathered again for the formal post-mortem that afternoon. It was a long and arduous process that took almost three hours. Sharon concluded that death had occurred within minutes of the victim being struck on the head, then stabbed. "I believe the weapon used in the stabbing was about four inches long and a quarter of an inch wide. She was hit on the head with a blunt object like a hammer. She was struck from the left side, suggesting that the killer was probably right-handed."

***

George studied the information that had started to flow in. House-to-house inquiries resulted in a clearer view of Linda's lifestyle. Her ex-husband had been traced and her parents contacted. The criminal records database showed that she had several convictions for drunkenness and disorderly conduct. The city's vice squad had advised that she was a known prostitute, and had been cautioned several times.

According to her mother, she had been a bubbly, intelligent child, but inclined to go her own way. She fell pregnant when she was seventeen and had two more children in quick succession.

"Linda couldn't settle down," her ex-husband's voice boomed from the recorder, as George replayed the tape of their interview. "She didn't have the self-discipline to adapt to marriage or motherhood. She liked her nights out with the girls too much and she liked other men even more. I begged her to stop, but she wouldn't. The last time she laughed at me, I left. I couldn't put up with her anymore.

"I tried to see the children as often as I could and I did my best to provide for them. I felt sorry for little Aisling; she was like a mother to the younger two. Linda was hopeless."

George knew inner city Dublin intimately. He had worked there for twenty years. He knew the streets, the alleys, the pubs and clubs. Dublin gave him his vast network of informants: the criminals who provided him with the tip-offs that made him the best-informed detective in the city.

He knew the wheelers and dealers, the con men, the thieves, the petty criminals, and the prostitutes. He also knew the serious criminals: the men who didn't think twice about taking a gun on an armed raid and using it. Over the years, he had locked up hundreds of criminals and earned himself a fierce reputation. He was seen as a hard and occasionally ruthless man, but always a great detective.

George moved easily among those who lived on the edge of what was legal. He drifted into pubs and nightclubs, exchanging glances with some thief or crook. Minutes apart, they'd meet in the gents where a fifty-euro note would be exchanged for a piece of paper or a whispered conversation.

Being a detective wasn't a job, it was a way of life for George. It was his drug of choice. He knew it, Gina knew it and his children knew it. Solving murders was his greatest professional high. Catching the perpetrators among the half million people who lived in Dublin took some doing.

He had been involved in thirty-five murders and had solved every one. Tough and uncompromising: people either loved or loathed him. He had few social graces and seldom apologised for anything.

George glanced at the clock that ticked loudly on his office wall. It was after midnight, and he had promised Gina he'd be home by ten. He sighed, and considered leaving, but the early stages of a murder inquiry had to take precedence over almost everything. Besides, what was the point? He'd just lie in bed, staring at the ceiling, thinking about the dead.

His mind was troubled by the fact that Linda Keenan, because she had sex for money, probably did not know her killer. The search for a man who killed with such frenzied violence was top priority.

George kept himself and his officers hard at it. He appealed through the local media for people to come forward; all those eyes and ears working for him and bringing him information was invaluable. He believed he was only a good detective because of everything people told him.

Tip-offs flooded the hotline and every detail was filed meticulously. Every tip generated more inquiries. Male friends--especially lovers--had to be traced, interviewed and eliminated; vehicle sightings had to be checked; and follow-up interviews arising from house-to-house inquiries had to be actioned.

A detailed picture of Linda's movements on the night she died began to emerge. She had left home at about 7p.m., telling Aisling that they were to stay in bed. She told them she was going to town and would be back later, while they were asleep. She kissed them goodbye and told them she'd see them in the morning.

From 7.30p.m. until 11p.m. she had been in several pubs. The last sighting of her was at 11.30p.m., when she had tried to hitch a lift by jumping out in front of a car. She was drunk. The lab report confirmed that her blood alcohol levels were dangerously high.

A witness came forward to report that he had seen Linda getting into a silver Passat estate. The driver had white hair and a full beard.

Investigators found an address book at Linda's house and began the task of locating her regular clients. George discreetly told the media they were searching for past boyfriends; experience had taught him that the public was rarely surprised at what happened to prostitutes. Thirty "boyfriends" were interviewed and eliminated. The usual checks had revealed nothing and they were still waiting for the driver of the Passat to come forward.

The vaginal swabs revealed no trace of semen, but there were traces of semen on the back of Linda's jeans. However, forensic scientists were unable to produce a blood group. Keeping details of the injuries secret, George announced to the public that the killer seemed to have had personal feelings towards Linda.

The crime scene investigators had amassed a large number of fingerprints at Linda's house, but they hadn't been able to eliminate a fragment of a fingerprint on the bathroom door knob. A purse that was missing from her handbag still hadn't been found.

A female police officer dressed up in Linda's clothes and a photograph of Linda's face was superimposed. Posters were distributed to supermarkets and businesses, but they resulted in no new leads. Almost two months after the murder, George's investigation was floundering.

Joanne Clancy

Chapter 3

"Is that George Ellis?" The woman on the other end of the line asked nervously.

"Who wants to know?" George asked in irritation, but his interest was piqued by the woman's soft London accent. He balanced the phone under his jaw, while trying to shove the endless pile of paperwork on his desk into some sort of order. He was almost an hour late for dinner and in no mood for another argument with Gina.

"I'm Miranda Hughes. I'm your mother."

The phone slipped from his tentative grasp, but he grabbed it just before it hit the desk. For a few moments, he couldn't speak. "That's impossible. My mother passed away last year." His voice came out in a croak, as he tried to swallow the lump in his throat. "You must be confusing me with someone else."

"I have information from your adoption file," she explained. "I sent you a letter and a photo."

"I didn't get them." He rummaged through the mess on his desk, silently cursing his lack of organisational skills. Eventually, he found the envelope with the neat, slanting handwriting addressed to Detective Chief Inspector George Ellis. He studied the words; as if he'd never seen his name before.

His childhood flashed before his eyes, and all the birthday parties, Christmases, cuts and bruises that his mom had kissed better. So many memories. Was this some sort of cruel joke? Anger surged through him.

With trembling fingers, he ripped open the envelope and stared at the photo clipped to the letter. He studied it, desperately trying to convince himself that she looked nothing like him, but there was no denying it; the truth stared back at him. They were the image of each other with the same world-weary grey eyes and high cheekbones.

Tears welled up in his eyes. He couldn't believe it. "Why are you coming forward now after all these years? I never even knew you existed."

"I'd like to tell you the truth about who you are and where you came from. I should have told you sooner.

"I never wanted to give you away, and I've always wanted to find you. You probably won't believe me, but I've always loved you." She took a deep breath before continuing. "My telephone number is in the letter. Call me when you've had a chance to read it. You deserve to know who you really are."

George switched on the desk lamp; he didn't want to miss a single detail. He had no idea what to think and no way of knowing how much that conversation would change the rest of his life.

Chapter 4

Nine weeks after Linda Keenan's murder, George was standing at the edge of a ghost estate: one of many housing estates that had been uncompleted or abandoned during the recession. Detective Sergeant Mike Byrne, powerfully built with a misleadingly trusting face, was waiting for him.

They'd been partners for more than fifteen years. Mike was the closest person to a friend that George would ever allow himself to have. He led George to a narrow lane between two houses. "A man walking his dog saw something lying in the grass at the end of the lane," Mike explained explained. "Initially, he assumed it was a shop mannequin. However, on closer inspection, he saw it was the body of a woman."

Walking carefully, George noticed the clear drag marks of disturbed gravel from the front of the lane to where the body lay. Tyre tracks in the muddy ground led from the roadway, along the back of the estate, and stopped close to the body.

There were also some patches of dried blood on the ground. He closed his eyes.

"Terrible location to die," Mike said.

George nodded, but didn't say anything. The wind picked up as they leant over the body. George pulled back the plastic sheet that partly covered the body of a woman in her mid-twenties. It was obvious that she had suffered severe head injuries.

She was sprawled on the grass, just in front of a pile of rubbish, with her head turned to the right. Her upper body was clothed in a cream cardigan; and a long, black wool coat covered her lower body. Her feet protruded beyond the end of the coat.

A cheap, black stiletto lay on the ground beside her left foot; the other shoe was a short distance away. There was a footprint on her thigh, similar to the footprint at the entrance to the laneway. Her face was smeared with mud, and blood stained the front of her cardigan. Small pools of coagulated blood soiled the ground above her head.

Her fake leather handbag lay open beside her. George pulled on his gloves and checked the bag. Inside, an address and telephone number had been scribbled on a piece of paper, which he handed to Mike to follow up.

George knelt down to examine the spot where the woman lay. He noticed that the blonde-haired woman had blue eyes and nicotine-stained fingers on her left hand. The exposed part of her body was cold to his touch. He shivered in the biting wind.

"It'll be difficult to preserve any contact trace-evidence in these conditions," Mike said as the rain squalled around them.

"Cover the body in plastic sheets and have it transported to the morgue," George said, getting to his feet. "Miss Tierney can conduct a more intensive examination there."

Task force officers had already begun an inch-by-inch fingertip search across the abandoned estate. They crawled on their hands and knees in the driving wind and rain as they painstakingly made their way along the ground. It was backbreaking work and George didn't envy them.

The address found in the handbag revealed that the dead woman was Rhona O' Farrell, and that she had applied for a job as a shop assistant the previous week. The shop owner provided the police with Rhona's home address: a run-down lodging house in the city centre. Apart from a few changes of clothes and two pairs of shoes, Rhona's entire wealth lay in the few coins she had in her purse.

Rhona was a lost soul. She was twenty-four years old, broke, and fending for herself. At sixteen, she ran away from home and for the next five years completely cut herself off from her family and friends. She hadn't even attended her mother's funeral. By the time she was twenty, she had two children by two different fathers. She could barely look after herself, let alone two babies, so she put them into foster care.

She worked as a cleaner at various hotels around the city to make ends meet. A month before her murder, she collected her wages and gave a week's notice, saying that she had to get away from a man she had been living with. Detectives learned that in the last few weeks of her life, she had been wandering the streets, almost destitute.

Severely depressed and down on her luck, Rhona had been hanging around the city's street corners. The landlady at the boarding house where she stayed had given her a room rent-free for a week, knowing that she was desperately trying to find another job.

On the night she died, she had spent a few hours getting ready to go out. George had noticed that she was wearing a considerable amount of eye make-up. Around 11.30p.m., a woman saw her getting into a strange man's car. Forensic lab results showed that she had had intercourse within twenty-four hours of her death.

George learned that a man driving a silver car had propositioned another woman on the same night. It was quite possible that the same man had picked up Rhona and taken her to the ghost estate.

The autopsy showed that there had been several blows to the victim's head. She had been dragged to the site where her body was found. Her clothes had been raised at the front, where she had been stabbed, then she had been turned over and more stab wounds inflicted. Her attacker had also trod on her thigh.

The nature of her injuries and the circumstances in which she had died, convinced George that the person who had murdered Linda Keenan had killed again.

Chapter 5

George quietly opened the front door. It was 6.30a.m. Gina was already up, making coffee. He looked at her for a moment, lovely as always in her cotton nightie and her hair curly from bed. He put his arms around her and kissed the back of her neck. She smelled of sleep, home and that intoxicatingly musky smell that was uniquely hers.

She shrugged away from him and reached for a bottle of water from the fridge. "Did you organise some time off? We should really visit Miranda. She's called a few times, asking when we're going to London. It's embarrassing having to put her off."

"Darling," he sighed, taking off his coat. "I can't, not now."

She gulped back the bottle of water and wiped her mouth on her sleeve. "Why not? You're not the only detective who can organise an investigation?"

George coughed. It was his tell: a sign that he was irritated. "I'm the head of the unit."

"You have a deputy."

"It's bad timing, love."

"It's always bad bloody timing." She crossed her arms and silently counted to three. "Do you even want to do this, George?"

"Of course I do."

"You look like hell. I'm worried about you. When was the last time you actually slept?"

He had no idea, but he knew his brain was addled. All he thought about was death and the faces of the murdered women.

"When's the last time you did anything other than work? I can't remember when we spent any time together as a family."

Gina was a freelance crime reporter. She worked part-time so she could be at home to look after their children. They lived in a grand old Georgian house in Howth with beautiful bay windows overlooking the harbor. It was a little run-down inside with scuffed floorboards, peeling paint and an overgrown garden that he kept meaning to get around to, but never seemed to have the time.

Gina had turned to him in bed one morning, propped up on her elbow, her hair messy and standing on end. The rain hammered against the window. "We need a holiday," she'd declared. Let's go somewhere."

"Where?"

"Somewhere. Anywhere. It doesn't matter, as long we're together. When was the last time we had a holiday?"

"We went to Dingle during the summer." He'd thought about the holiday they'd taken with her parents. They'd rented a cottage on the edge of the peninsula. The photos showed four smiling adults and two happy children, but it had been a nightmare. George had been withdrawn and preoccupied with work, and Gina had been cranky and exhausted from running around after the children.

George had lain on his back and stared at the ceiling, listening to the rain outside. Then he had turned to look at her. "Are you happy?"

"I don't know anymore."

His heart pounded in his chest.

"Sometimes days pass without us exchanging more than a few words. You're out the door at the crack of dawn and you're rarely home before midnight. I miss you."

"I miss you too."

George adored his wife. She was his rock, his anchor. He had no idea what he'd do without her. "What are we going to do?"

"You should take some time off. I don't mean a week or two. We should go away for six months, travel, hire a campervan and rent out the house."

"What about the kids?"

"They'll love it."

"Where would we go?"

"France, Spain, Portugal. We'll just drive around Europe. I speak French and you speak fluent Spanish. It wouldn't even cost that much, really."

He sat up and smiled slightly. "I've always loved The Algarve."

"I want to taste real French bread and pastries and red wine and cheese."

"We'll have to organise passports for the kids. It would be the first time they'd left Ireland."

He had rubbed his hand over his tired eyes. "Let's do it."

She had laughed and kissed him and they had made love as if they were already gone. That had been nearly six months ago…

Now, he stood in the kitchen, looking at her, demented from lack of sleep. "I'll take some time off soon. I'll sort it."

Gina rolled her eyes. She'd heard it all before. "Please, George. It's important." He knew it was about more than a holiday. "I promise."

"We can't go on like this."

"I know, you're right. We'll talk later." He kissed her on the cheek and dragged himself upstairs. His phone rang. "I'm on my way." He splashed water on his face, brushed his teeth and pulled on a clean shirt.

"I have to go." He kissed Gina goodbye. "Everything will be fine." Then he slammed the door behind him and disappeared once again.

Chapter 6

George issued a dark warning to the public via the media. "I believe the person we are looking for will kill again. He is a sadistic killer and quite possibly a sexual pervert. These women were killed with a maniacal viciousness.

"He is obviously mentally ill and could flip at any moment. Look at your husbands, boyfriends, brothers and father. Ask yourself if he could be the man we're searching for. Maybe he lives in your house or down the street. He lives somewhere, he works for someone, and someone out there knows this man. It is imperative that we catch him before he kills again."

The murder of two prostitutes within a few months caused some women to stop soliciting. Others said they had no choice and had to accept the dangers. Reports came in about other attacks on women in the city, and while each was carefully investigated, none could be connected to the murders of Linda Keenan or Rhona O' Farrell.

Fear among women in the city was palpable. Hardware stores reported a run on door locks and safety chains. Almost a hundred calls a day flooded the incident room, and each call was painstakingly followed up.

Months had passed, and George's investigation was going nowhere. He had tried everything to push the inquiry forward, but it was like hunting for a ghost. Every line of inquiry had been followed up. Dodgy punters were closely questioned, but it resulted in nothing. Prostitutes were asked to identify clients who could have been capable of two brutal murders. Numerous men were checked. Nothing.

George was fully aware of the cruel paradox: if he had any chance of catching the killer, more clues and new lines of inquiry were needed, which would only be forthcoming if the killer struck again. George could only wait.

Chapter 7

Gina squeezed her husband's hand as the plane descended towards London Heathrow. George stared out the window, knowing that in less than an hour he would meet his birth mother for the first time. His stomach was in knots as he looked at the soft white clouds.

His life and everything he had believed to be true had been turned upside down. His adoptive parents had given him unconditional love and acceptance, but he wondered why they hadn't told him the truth about his past, and now it was too late to ask. Maybe Miranda could answer some of the questions that plagued him.

He wiped his sweaty palms on his jeans as the plane came in to land. Although he wanted to meet his mother, he had to fight the urge to run away. His heart raced when he caught sight of her at the far end of the arrivals terminal. She was tall and her hair was longer and darker than in the photo she had sent. She was anxiously searching each passenger's face for her son. Her expression reflected the same nervous excitement that George was feeling.

He quickened his pace and as soon as he saw her, he knew she was his mother. Miranda reached out to him and hugged him close. When she stepped back, her eyes were full of unshed tears as she took in every detail of his face.

"George," she whispered, her voice shaking. "My baby. My son."

Her words sounded strange to him; only one woman had ever called him her son, and now she was gone.

"I'm Gina, George's wife." Gina stepped forward to shake Miranda's hand.

"It's lovely to meet you, Gina." Miranda smiled nervously and Gina couldn't help feeling sorry for her. George wasn't a good communicator at the best of times, and now he was at a complete loss for words.

Gina did her best to make small talk with Miranda as she drove the thirty miles from Heathrow to her home in St. Alban's. "Weren't the Harry Potter films and Goldeneye set in St. Alban's?" Gina asked, as they sped along the motorway.

"Yes, that's right. It's quite a diverse city. I've lived there for twenty years and you couldn't pay me to move."

From his vantage point on the back seat, George stole glances at his mother. In her early sixties, she was slim and attractive. Her lightly tanned skin enhanced her lovely eyes and dark hair.

Before long, they arrived at Miranda's Victorian house, where they were staying for the weekend. Gina marvelled at the bay windows and classic rendered façade. "You have a beautiful home," she said as Miranda showed them inside.

"Thank you," Miranda smiled gratefully at her. "You should freshen up while I make a start on dinner."

They kept the conversation light throughout the evening. Gina went to bed early so that mother and son could be alone. A few glasses of wine helped to ease the tension between George and Miranda. He had so much he wanted to say to her, so many questions to ask, but it was difficult to cram a lifetime of emotions and experiences into a few short days.

They sat in silence for a while, until eventually Miranda reached for his hand. "I'm glad you're here," she said.

They stayed up until the early hours of the morning. Neither of them could believe what was happening.

Finally, George asked her the question that they had been dancing around all evening. "Miranda…mom…who is my birth father?"

She sat up straight in her chair and cleared her throat. He could see she was nervous. "His name was Oliver. It was a long time ago and a difficult time in my life. I was so young when I met him. I've repressed most of my memories about him. I had to, otherwise I wouldn't have survived."

"What do you mean?"

"I was only sixteen when I met Oliver. I was young and impressionable. The 1960s wasn't a good time to be unmarried and pregnant. I didn't want to give you up, but it was my only option."

George held her hand as tears welled in her eyes.

"You were two months old when Oliver took you out for a few hours. I almost died when he returned without you. He said he'd left you at a somewhere safe, but he refused to tell me where."

He sat in silence, trying to take in everything she was saying. Eventually, they were too tired to talk any longer, and for the first time in his life, he kissed his mother good night.

He tossed and turned in bed, desperate to know more about his birth father. The more he thought about him, the more he wanted to meet him and hear his side of the story. Maybe his father's memories would be clearer than Miranda's. Maybe he would tell him why he had left him at the church that day.

However, knowing isn't always better. Sometimes, the past should be left in the past, especially when the truth changes everything…

PART 2

1968

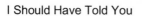

I Should Have Told You

Chapter 8

Oliver Higgins stared out the window, waiting for inspiration to strike. Usually, the busy little café provided the perfect backdrop to his writing. It was where he came for company, coffee, and to eavesdrop on the conversations going on around him, but that afternoon was an exception. No matter how hard he tried, he couldn't get the ideas in his head to translate into words.

Absentmindedly, he tapped his pen against the table and gazed at the people as they clambered off the bus that had just pulled up outside. A striking young woman jumped off the last step and immediately caught his eye. Her dark, bobbed hair shone in the afternoon sun as she headed straight for the café.

"Hi," he said, standing behind her in the queue. He flashed his most charming smile at her.

"Hi," she replied, before turning to the waitress to place her order.

"I can highly recommend the apple pie," he said. "I'm Oliver, by the way."

"I'm Miranda," she smiled shyly up at him, taking in his rugged good looks, flattered by the attention of an older man.

"I'll get this," he said, handing a note to the waitress. "Won't you join me?"

Miranda followed him to his table in the corner by the window. Oliver sat down and gazed into her clear, grey eyes that looked at him so innocently. He had a weakness for attractive women, the younger the better, and she was prettier than most. He watched as she ate the apple pie and sipped her coffee.

"Today's my birthday," she said in between bites.

"Happy birthday, Miranda," he smiled.

"Can you guess my age?" She grinned mischievously.

"It's impolite to ask a lady her age," he replied in the English accent he liked to affect.

"You're not asking; I want you to guess."

"Twenty-two."

"No, I'm sixteen."

"Impossible," he whispered.

"Yes, sixteen today," she giggled.

He wondered if he should leave, but one glance into her eyes convinced him to stay. It was love at first sight.

Miranda was enthralled as he told her about his travels around Europe and his childhood in London. He spoke about literature, art and his passion for writing. He treated her like an equal, not like the other adults in her life.

"It's late," she said with regret, glancing at her watch. "I should head home before my mother starts worrying. It's getting dark already."

"I'll walk with you. Where do you live?"

"Don't worry about me. I'll be fine. I live just across the park." She stood up. Oliver walked her to the door and watched as she crossed the road. She turned and waved at him before disappearing into the darkness.

The following afternoon, Oliver arrived at the café earlier than usual, hoping to meet the loveliest girl he had ever seen. He spent most of the afternoon watching the passersby as they went about their business, scanning the crowds for a glimpse of Miranda.

Killaloe in County Clare was a busy town and a popular spot with tourists and locals alike. It was the capital of Ireland's inland waterways and was renowned for its history and fishing. He had spent many happy afternoons fishing on Lough Derg, but not that day; that day he had his eye on an entirely different catch.

His heart stood still as the bus pulled up across the street. He glanced at his watch; it was 4.15p.m.: the same time as when he'd seen her the previous day. He watched as the passengers climbed down the steps. Finally, there she was again: his beautiful, innocent Miranda. He dashed across the road and called out to her as she headed towards the park. Her face lit up as soon as she saw him.

"What are you doing here?" she asked.

"I was in the café, and I saw you. I'll walk you home."

"No, my father would be angry if he saw us."

"We won't let him see us," Oliver grinned. He took her arm and walked her towards the harbour, where the boats were moored.

A quiver of excitement shot through her as they walked past the gates of the park. Oliver made her feel special, not like the boys at school who were silly and immature. Already, she was counting down the days until she could leave.

However, school was a welcome distraction from the constant bickering at home. She hated the way her father constantly insulted her mother. Depressed and hopeless, her mother had nothing left to give her daughter. Miranda promised herself that she would never be with a man like that.

Miranda was hungry for love and Oliver was more than willing to give her the attention she craved. He spoke to her like an equal, as if her opinion mattered. No one had ever made her feel like that. He kissed her on the cheek before leaving her at the edge of the park. She liked that he was her own private secret.

She stood on her tiptoes and kissed him. "Will I see you tomorrow?" she asked.

"I hope so."

She smiled and swung her schoolbag over her shoulder, almost skipping down the street. She had never been so happy, but she was too innocent to wonder why a man of Oliver's age would be interested in her or to ask questions about his past.

Chapter 9

"I don't want you to go home," Oliver said as he pulled her behind a tree. "I hate it when we're apart."

"Me too," Miranda said.

He held her close and kissed her. "Let's run away. Let's get married."

She pulled away, shocked. "Seriously?"

"Absolutely. I love you. I want to be with you. Will you marry me?"

"When? How?"

"Don't worry about the details. I'll take care of everything. Meet me tomorrow at 6p.m. I'll wait for you by the old oak tree. Pack a suitcase. This will be the adventure of a lifetime. Will you come with me?"

Miranda hesitated for a moment. She had only known him a few months, but she believed he loved her. She wasn't certain that she loved him, but she liked how she felt around him. He was kinder to her than anyone else in her life was, and she was sure that she would be leaving her family for a better life with him. She threw her arms around him. "Of course," she laughed. "What will I tell my parents?"

"Forget about them. I'll see you tomorrow."

He kissed her again and watched as she walked away.

***

Oliver waited impatiently behind the tall oak tree near Miranda's house. He glanced at his watch; already, it was 6.10p.m. She was ten minutes late. He was completely focused on her house. From his vantage point, he would see her as soon as she stepped outside. He prayed that her mother wouldn't follow her.

He watched as the front door opened and Miranda appeared. When he saw the suitcase in her hand, he breathed a deep sigh of relief. He hadn't been sure that she would go through with his plan. It was all he could do not to run across the road to her, but he didn't want to risk anyone spotting him.

"Hurry," he whispered, kissing her before grabbing her suitcase. They walked quickly to the far side of the park, where Oliver had parked his car. "Jump in," he said, throwing her little suitcase on the backseat.

"This is exciting!" Miranda said, clapping her hands. "I can't believe we're actually running away together. It's so romantic."

At Shannon Airport, anticipation fluttered in her stomach as she walked up the steps of the plane. It was her first flight, and she could hardly sit still. She stared in wonder at the fluffy white clouds, while Oliver smiled indulgently at her, enjoying her excitement.

London was everything that Miranda had imagined and more. The 1960s revolution was in full swing, and London was the world capital of cool. She was enthralled by the heady combination of affluence and youth. She loved the fashion boutiques that lined the King's Road, especially Bazaar, Mary Quant's iconic store, where radical miniskirts were flying off the rails.

She fell in with the creative set that gravitated to the capital city: the artists, writers, magazine publishers, photographers, and musicians. London was a melting pot of all things hip and fashionable. She loved every minute of it.

London was everything that Oliver had promised and more. When he wasn't writing, they explored London together: the hot spots of Carnaby Street, Big Ben, the Houses of Parliament and Buckingham Palace. She happily followed him as he went from one market stall to another at The Old Covent Garden market, where he searched for old books and documents, while she joyously absorbed the sounds, smells and sights of her new world.

I Should Have Told You

Chapter 10

"I'm pregnant," Miranda announced. Her voice trembled.

Oliver stared at her; having a child was the last thing he wanted. He forced a smile and hugged her.

"I want to go home."

"This is your home now."

"I miss my mother." She swallowed the lump in her throat.

"Stop whining," Oliver snapped. "We'll be fine." His tone invited no argument. This wasn't the charming man she knew, and for the first time she felt afraid.

She went into the bedroom and burst into tears. She didn't want to be pregnant. She thought about calling her mother, but she knew Oliver would be angry.

They spent more and more time in their cramped apartment; Oliver was trying to finish his novel and he didn't want her going out alone. Miranda tried to be happy about her pregnancy, but Oliver's indifference was upsetting.

She did her best to please him: cooking, cleaning and not asking any questions when he went out alone late at night, his hat pulled low over his eyes. Nothing she did worked. He told her every day that he loved her, but his words quickly lost their meaning when he insulted her growing belly.

Baby George was born on August 2nd, 1969. Miranda had no idea how to care for a newborn. Money was running low. Oliver hadn't met his publisher's deadline, and he'd already spent his advance. He convinced Miranda to take a job as a waitress, while he stayed home with George and wrote.

She worked hard to earn enough money for George's baby formula and to keep Oliver supplied with the whiskey he enjoyed. Her only friend in the big city was Victor Elliott, a little old man who lived in the ground floor apartment. Every night, he waited up for her, braving the elements to make sure she arrived home safely. Relief flooded through her as soon as she saw his fragile body silhouetted by the dim porch light. Oliver never waited up for her; he was usually passed out in bed by the time she got home.

The old man always met her with a beaming smile that creased his weatherworn face. He'd take her by the arm and ask her how her night had gone. He couldn't help worrying about her. Ever since she'd moved into the apartment upstairs with the strange man she called her husband, he had worried about her.

Victor didn't trust him. He knew evil when he saw it and he could see the devil in Oliver's eyes. Oliver scared him, and the old man didn't scare easily.

Chapter 11

Miranda carefully inserted the key in the lock, praying that the squeaky door wouldn't wake Oliver. She tiptoed across the threadbare carpet to the large old chest of drawers, which was George's bed. George was lying inside with blue-tinged lips. He was hardly breathing.

She grabbed her baby and cradled him in her arms, frantically rocking him back and forth. Awakened by his cries, Oliver watched jealously.

"How could you do this to your own son?" Miranda demanded.

"I'm tired of hearing him wailing all day long."

Miranda stared at him, but didn't say anything. She knew better than to answer back. Oliver had become increasingly hot-tempered since the baby's birth, and she had seen the signs of his cruelty to George: blood on his nose and a cut on his forehead. She wanted to stay at home, terrified that Oliver would kill their son, but he insisted that she went to work.

"We have to get rid of him," Oliver announced, swinging around in his chair.

"What do you mean?" Miranda cried.

"I can't stand much more of his incessant crying. He's driving me mad."

Miranda ran into the hall, clutching George to her, petrified of what Oliver might do. She had to find a way to keep him away from his father. She wished that life could go back to the way it had been when they'd first moved to London.

She tried to be a good mother, but with little money, buying formula and nappies had become a problem, and being hungry made the baby cry even more. Oliver was becoming increasingly jealous of any attention she showed their son, and her life was quickly becoming a living nightmare. She crept downstairs, hoping that Victor was still awake.

"What happened?" the old man asked, as soon as he saw her.

"Nothing." She sniffed, brushing the tears from her eyes.

"What a handsome chap," Victor cooed, putting out his finger for George to hold.

"He's beautiful." She couldn't help smiling through her tears.

"You certainly have your hands full."

"I don't know what to do."

"Do what's in your heart; that's what my father always told me."

She stared down the street as she gently rocked her son. Part of her still loved London, but the hell inside her apartment was becoming more and more difficult to handle. She was too afraid to defend herself or George against Oliver's violent outbursts, but she was also afraid of being alone in the city without him.

Eventually, she dared to venture back inside. Oliver wrapped his arms around her and buried his face in her hair. "I'm sorry, babe. You know how much I love you."

She hugged him back. "I love you too," she whispered. "I'll feed George, and then I'm all yours."

The following morning, Miranda awoke with a jolt.

"Where's the money you earned last night?" Oliver demanded, rifling through her purse.

She sat up in bed and rubbed the sleep from her eyes.

"It's in my coat pocket."

"What it doing in there?" he yelled, flinging her purse on the bed.

She looked around anxiously and saw George wrapped in blankets on the couch. She jumped out of bed to pick him up.

"Leave him. I'm taking him to a better home than this," Oliver said.

"No, please let me keep him. I promise I'll keep him quiet."

"No! I'm tired of him. All he does is cry." Oliver picked him up roughly. "I want my old life back."

Miranda was no match for his strength. There was no point putting up a fight. Oliver hated their baby, and that was that. She blinked away her tears as she handed him a bottle. "He doesn't need that now," Oliver said firmly, walking towards the door.

Miranda put the pacifier in her son's mouth, praying that it would stop him crying. She bent to kiss George goodbye, but Oliver pushed her away. He slammed the door on his way out, and Miranda sank to the floor.

Chapter 12

Oliver held George close to his chest as the wind picked up. His son's thin blanket did little to keep him warm. Not for the first time, Oliver was grateful for the anonymity that the busy city provided. No one even glanced at him as he hurried down the steps to Charing Cross Tube Station and boarded the underground train.

Within a few minutes, the train pulled out of the station. The gentle rocking motion quickly lulled George to sleep. Oliver held him as he slept, by all appearances a caring father. An hour later, the train screeched to a halt.

Oliver stood up and quickly exited the train. He looked around for the perfect spot. Fallen leaves crunched underfoot as he walked. He stopped outside a sign for The Rising Sun Apartments and made his way around the back of the three-storey building. The rear garden was hidden from view by a huge old oak tree that towered over the property, providing the seclusion he needed.

He held his breath as he pushed open the door and walked into the building unseen. There were two doors on either side of the narrow hall, and a winding staircase straight ahead of him. He climbed the stairs and arrived onto a landing.

He wrapped the grubby blanket tightly around his son and laid him on the floor, making sure the pacifier was firmly in his mouth. Then, he turned and left, without a second thought.

***

"What have you done with my son?" Miranda wailed. "Where is he? I want my baby."

"He's fine," Oliver insisted. "I left him in a safe place where someone would find him. A family who can afford to take care of him will adopt him. Stop your ridiculous crying."

Miranda didn't believe him. She knew how much he hated the baby and decided that it was time to escape.

***

Susan Ellis strolled home, enjoying the last of the autumn sunshine. It was Friday evening, and she had just finished work for the day. The weekend stretched out ahead of her, and she was looking forward to spending some quality time with her husband. As much as she loved teaching, it was always a relief when the Friday afternoon school bell rang at 4p.m. to signal the end of another week.

She smiled as she climbed the few steps to her apartment at The Rising Sun, pausing at the post box to retrieve her mail. Just as she turned the key in the lock, she heard a baby crying. She ran upstairs. Her heart stood still when she saw the child lying on the cold, tiled floor.

Joanne Clancy

He was crying and kicking his little feet. His blanket and pacifier were beside him. She picked him up and looked around to see if his parents were nearby. The comforting warmth of her touch stopped his cries. Susan knew that none of the other residents had children, and there was no one else around. She returned to her apartment and immediately called the police.

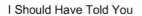

I Should Have Told You

Chapter 13

"I wonder how my baby's doing," Susan said to her husband as she sipped her first cup of coffee of the day. She hadn't slept much during the night, worrying about the little boy. She and her husband had been trying for a baby for several years, and she had already started to think of the abandoned child as her own.

"He's in good hands," David reassured her. "The hospital will make sure he goes to a good home."

"We should try to adopt him," Susan suggested.

The phone rang before David had a chance to reply. "Are you the woman who found the baby?" asked the man on the other end of the line.

"Yes, I found him," Susan replied. "Who are you?"

The man didn't answer. "The baby's mother couldn't take care of him."

"Are you his father?"

"Yes."

"Where are you?"

"The baby's mother wants him back. She'll be at the hospital this afternoon to get him." Then the line went dead.

Susan immediately called the police, who were already checking the birth certificates of all white males born between January and October 1969. However, nothing matched the baby's footprints, and Miranda never showed up at the hospital to collect her son.

Chapter 14

Tears streamed down Miranda's face as she signed the adoption papers. She had no other choice; her mother refused to let her come home unless she gave up her son, and she had nowhere else to go.

"It's for the best," Mrs. Hughes said, patting her daughter on the shoulder. "I'm sure he'll go to a good home, and you can put this whole sorry mess behind you."

Miranda couldn't control her tears as she waited for someone to bring her baby to her one last time. Just when she thought she couldn't stand waiting a second longer, the door opened, and the social worker arrived, holding George in her arms. "You have fifteen minutes," the social worker said solemnly.

Miranda lifted her son and covered his chubby face with kisses. He grabbed a handful of her hair, but didn't pull, holding it in his tiny hands.

"Mummy loves you," she whispered. "I'll always love you."

The door opened too soon, signalling that their time together was over. Miranda screamed and held her son tighter. "Please don't take him," she begged.

"I'm sorry," the social worker said, reaching for the child.

"No, please don't take my baby. You can't have him. I'm not letting him go. I'll be a good mother, I promise. He needs me. He's crying. He needs his mother."

Mrs. Hughes held her daughter by the shoulders, while the social worker pried the baby from her arms.

"Mummy loves you," Miranda cried. "I'm sorry, George. I'm so sorry. I'll come back for you, I promise."

With one final pull, her baby was wrenched away. In his tiny hand, he clutched a few strands of his mother's hair. The door closed and Miranda held her breath, listening intently to his cries as he was taken away. Then she covered her face with her hands and sobbed.

Chapter 15

February 14th, 1970
County Clare, Ireland

"Happy Valentine's Day, darling."

Miranda froze at the sound of Oliver's voice.

"Please meet me at our café. I miss you. I'm so sorry for what happened. I promise I'll get our son back. I love you."

She took a deep breath. "Don't ever call me again! I never want to see you." She slammed down the phone, no longer the naive girl that he had once known. A sense of power and fearlessness flowed through her. Finally, she felt free.

Oliver was heartbroken and furious. He jumped in his car and started to drive. He drove for miles, not knowing where he was going. Hours later, exhausted and hungry, he pulled up outside a busy restaurant to get something to eat.

He was just about to get out of the car, when he saw her. He stared out the windscreen as the blood drained from his face. The woman looked just like Miranda. Even her dark hair was styled in the same, sleek bob. He watched her intently as she locked her car and stopped outside the restaurant to read the menu.

Then the rage of Miranda's rejection hit him. He looked around to see if anyone was watching and quickly walked towards the woman's car, which was parked across the street. He opened the bonnet and pulled on the ignition coil until he loosened it completely. Satisfied that the car wouldn't start, he climbed back into his car and waited.

Norah Ryan, a twenty-one-year-old legal secretary, was unaware that someone was watching her. An hour later, Oliver watched as Norah got into her car and put the key in the ignition. The car didn't start. She kept trying until the battery ran down.

It was time.

Oliver emerged from the shadows and tapped on her window. "Do you need any help?" he asked, flashing his beguiling smile.

Norah looked at him for a moment. He had a pleasant face and she quickly decided she could trust him. "The car won't start," she said, opening the door. "It's always playing up. She smiled apologetically up at him.

"Don't worry. I'm sure we'll have it fixed in no time." He winked conspiratorially at her before opening the bonnet and fiddling with the wires. "Try it again."

He chatted with her as he worked on the car, his charming manner easing any doubts she felt. "I'd be happy to give you a lift home in my car," he offered. "I'm parked just down the road."

Fooled by the handsome stranger, Norah accepted. As they walked towards the edge of the village, darkness hid them from view. Oliver paused at the isolated spot beside a church. "It's time," he said, turning towards her.

"Time for what?" Norah asked, oblivious to the danger she was in.

"For you to die."

She didn't have time to react before he began stabbing her, burying the three inch blade over and over again into her body. It was retribution for a betrayal that the young woman knew nothing about.

However, Norah was a fighter. She clawed at his face, drawing blood. She held his wrist so tight that when he drew back to stab her again, she tore his watch off. Nothing worked. There was no escape for her. He was too strong and kept up his deranged stabbing until he was satisfied.

He gazed at the wounds that covered her face and body, and at the blood that saturated the ground beneath her. Then, he turned and walked away, relieved that he had exorcised his demons.

Calmly, he walked back up the street into the village, huddled deep into his coat, his hat pulled low over his eyes. He climbed into his car, unaware of the clues he had left behind: his watch, his shoeprint and his palm print on the driver's door of Norah's car.

However, the investigators couldn't connect any of the clues with a suspect. There was no apparent motive, and she hadn't been robbed. The key to her car was still in the ignition. She was fully clothed, and there were no signs of a sexual assault. However, the police knew that it had to be personal somehow; forty knife wounds was overkill.

Oliver was beginning to unravel. His thirst for revenge was all-consuming, and his need to kill again escalated as the months dragged by. He moved to Dublin, believing that the busy capital city would offer him the anonymity he required.

He loved the freedom he had in Dublin to prowl for victims whenever he chose and basked in his deranged belief that he held the life of everyone he saw in his hands. It was an addictive feeling for the narcissistic killer. Murder gave him the power he craved.

Chapter 16

Eileen Duffy was singing along to the car radio, trying to stay awake on the four-hour drive from her parents' house in County Kerry to the house she shared in Dublin with two other nurses. She hated driving alone at night on the motorway, and she couldn't help feeling nervous about the car that had been following her for almost an hour. At first, she tried to blame her fears on her over-active imagination, but eventually she decided to slow down so the driver would overtake her.

Oliver was driving back to Dublin from Killaloe, when he noticed the pretty brunette stopped at the traffic lights in front of him. He followed her on the motorway towards Dublin, wondering how he would get her attention.

There were no other cars around when he flashed his headlights and blew the horn several times, doing his best to make her stop. It was past midnight on a Sunday, and most people were already in bed. The roads were deserted, just the way he liked them.

Thinking that the driver might actually be trying to let her know that something was wrong with her car, Eileen decided to stop. Oliver pulled up just in front of her. "Your back tyre looks a bit loose," he said, approaching the car. "I've been trying to flag you down for a while."

"Sorry." Her nerves eased when she realised that the harmless looking man had only been trying to help her.

"No problem. I'll do my best to fix it for you."

She watched while he returned to his car and grabbed his tools, then knelt down by the tyre and pretended to tighten the wheel nuts.

"Thanks so much," she said, relief flooding through her. She made a silent promise to herself not to drive alone at night again.

"Don't mention it." He wiped his hands on his trousers and headed back to his car, while she started her car and attempted to drive away. The car lurched to a stop within a few metres, just as he knew it would. She got out and checked what had happened.

He watched in his rearview mirror and quickly made a U-turn, parking his car alongside her. "Hop in. I'll drive you to the nearest service station. I think there's one a few miles up the road."

She looked around, realising that she was stuck in the dark, in the middle of nowhere. With a stifled sigh, she knew she didn't have any other option.

They passed the first service station, but it was closed. Suddenly, Oliver pulled off the motorway onto country roads.

"Where are you going?"

"You'll see," he replied, cryptically.

Although he seemed friendly, her stomach somersaulted. She started talking, as much to calm her own fears as to gauge the stranger's mood. "What do you do for a living?" she asked, forcing a brightness she didn't feel.

"I'm a writer."

"What sort of books do you write?"

"Murder mysteries."

His answer did nothing to alleviate her building fears. She decided to stop talking and focused instead on finding an opportunity to escape. Silently, she prayed he would stop the car. She watched him from the corner of her eye, doing her best to memorise his face. A stop sign loomed in front of them. To her utter relief, he slowed down.

She leapt from the car and ran as fast as she could through the nearby field. Glancing over her shoulder, she saw that the stranger was still in his car, but he had switched off the lights. She could feel him watching her, contemplating his next move.

She kept on running until she reached another road and flagged down a passing car. It was 3.15a.m.

Oliver waited for her to disappear from sight. Then he drove back to her car, carefully wiped away his prints, and disappeared once again into the night.

I Should Have Told You

Joanne Clancy

Part 3

2014

I Should Have Told You

Chapter 17

"I want to find my father," George said hesitantly. He had resisted asking too many questions about his father, afraid of damaging their fledgling relationship. He knew she didn't want to talk about him, but George had to know.

"If that's what you want, I will do everything in my power to help you find him."

"Thank you," George said, hugging her. "I just want to meet him."

"No matter what you discover, I want you to remember that nothing your father did was because of you. At the end of our relationship, he hated me, not you."

"What do you mean?" Clearly, she was trying to protect him from what she already knew about his father. "Whatever he did couldn't have been that bad. Why did he hate you?"

"He was a complicated man." Her voice trailed off.

"Whatever he might have done, he's still my father."

"I know." She started crying. "This is so upsetting. I don't want to cause any trouble for you. Maybe you should drop the whole thing and let your father go."

"I can't. He's out there somewhere, and I need to meet him, or at least know why I shouldn't."

"I understand, but I don't even know where to look for him."

"Leave that to me," George grinned. "I've picked up a few detective skills over the years."

***

George sat at his computer, waiting impatiently for the email to open. His mother had gone through some old boxes in the attic and had discovered a photo of his father. It took forever for the large file to download, and his anxiety increased with every minute that ticked by. At long last, he was about to see his father's face.

Finally, his head and shoulders appeared. He stared at the photo of the man who looked nothing like what his mother had described. Miranda had said he was handsome with warm brown eyes. Instead, an emotionless face with dark, dead eyes stared back at him.

"He has the face of a murderer," Gina said, peering over her husband's shoulder.

"Don't be daft," George snapped, but he could see what she meant. Oliver Higgins did not look like a good person.

The more he studied the photo, the more he saw the resemblances between them: the same hairline, strong jawline and cleft chin, even the shape of their eyes was the same. He shivered involuntarily as he looked into his father's eyes.

Deep down, he was conflicted. Something didn't feel right, and for the first time he wondered if he should stop digging up the past and give up on trying to find him.

I Should Have Told You

Chapter 18

It was February 12th, two days before Valentine's Day, as twenty-year old Ciara Dixon waved her friends goodnight and began walking home to the house she shared with her boyfriend. The freezing fog had enveloped her by the time she realised that she was being followed. She glanced over her shoulder and peered through the mist, but could barely make out the outline of a broad-shouldered man.

Her heart pounded as she quickened her pace, wondering which path to take; she wanted to avoid walking by the river. She stuck to the middle of the footpath, walking quickly past the lonely laneways between the housing estates. Relief flooded through her when she saw the row of houses where she lived.

Suddenly, she was struck across the back of her head. She fell to her knees and started screaming. Her attacker clamped his hand over her mouth.

"Shut up!" he hissed in her ear. She immediately noticed the London twang in his accent. She screamed again and he punched her on the back of her head, before pushing her against the wall.

"What the hell's going on down there?" A man's voice pierced the darkness. He opened his bedroom window to see what all the noise was about. Then he ran downstairs to help, but the attacker had already run off.

Ciara sat on the kerb. Within a few minutes, she felt something warm and sticky on her hands. They were covered in blood. Then she really started screaming. An ambulance quickly arrived on the scene and rushed her to hospital.

George strode through the sliding doors into the Emergency Room. He approached the desk and showed his badge to the nurse on duty. "I'm looking for Ciara Dixon."

The nurse glanced at the monitor in front of her. "She's in cubicle twelve."

George nodded his thanks and weaved his way through the waiting area, blocking out the groans of the binge drinkers, the drug addicts, and the beaten women.

He paused outside Ciara's cubicle, before sweeping the heavy curtain aside. A pale girl, with her head bandaged and eyes closed, was propped up against the pillows. She looked tiny and fragile as a bird. A middle-aged man sat slumped in a chair by the bed, snoring gently.

George coughed. The man jumped to attention, his grey hair standing on end. "Who the hell are you?" he demanded.

"I'm DCI George Ellis. I'd like to ask your daughter a few questions."

"Can't it wait?"

"It's okay, Dad. I'll talk to him," Ciara insisted, turning bruised, bloodshot eyes towards George.

He took in the sight of the girl. She had needed emergency neurosurgery; lacerations to her head had caused compound fractures to her skull. Surgeons had removed a sliver of bone from her brain and her head was swaddled in heavy bandages.

Privately, George was convinced that she was the killer's latest victim. Her injuries were too similar to those of the other women for it to have been anyone else.

"Can you describe your attacker?" George asked, getting straight down to business.

"He was quite athletic in build, about six feet tall, but he was wearing a balaclava over his face."

"You were lucky."

"I don't feel particularly lucky," Ciara snapped, her big blue eyes huge in her pale face.

I Should Have Told You

Chapter 19

Spring soon gave way to summer, and George was no closer to catching the killer. The sun blazed down from perfect blue skies. Laundry dried quickly on clothes lines, reservoirs emptied, drought warnings were issued, and July was the hottest month on record.

Twelve kilometres from Dublin City, in the seaside village of Dalkey, lived the O' Sullivan family. Long Meadow Farm had been in the family for almost two hundred years , and it was there that Janice and Aidan O' Sullivan raised their daughters: fourteen year old Deirdre and fifteen-year-old Iona.

There were only a few days left before the summer holidays ended and the new school year began. The sisters went to visit their friends in the village with strict instructions from their mother to be home by 10p.m. on what she knew would be a clear, moonlit night.

"Come on, Dee," Iona said, trying to drag her sister away from their friends. "Mom will go crazy if we're late."

"Okay, okay. Go on ahead of me, I won't be long. I'll catch up with you," Dee said, hanging back to say goodbye to her friends.

As it was a clear, warm night Janice wasn't concerned when Iona arrived home without her sister. Deirdre was the chatterbox of the two; it was always "five more minutes" with her. Besides, the girls had walked along that country lane alone many times.

Meanwhile, Deirdre was struggling to catch up with her sister. Her feet ached as she tottered uphill in her tight high-heeled sandals. As she leaned against a fence to take off her sandals and massage her feet, she noticed a stranger walking up the lane towards her. He reminded her of her grandfather with his shock of thick white hair.

"Hello," he glanced quickly at her as he drew level, before walking on.

"Hi," Deirdre smiled up at him. She wasn't afraid and assumed he was staying in the nearby holiday homes. Her biggest concern was to get home quickly so her mother wouldn't be too annoyed. Sighing, she slipped on her sandals and continued walking. She was surprised when she caught up with the stranger.

"Hello again," he smiled. "It's a lovely evening."

"It certainly is," she smiled back at him as they walked together.

"Do you have far to go?" he asked.

"About a kilometre."

"Why isn't your boyfriend walking you home?"

"He's working in the village pub tonight."

They continued walking in silence for a while. The stranger kept blowing his nose. "I have a summer cold," he apologised. "There's nothing worse."

Deirdre nodded. The man stopped to tie his shoelace, and she waited for him.

"Well, this is home," she said when they reached the gate to Long Meadow Farm.

She turned to wish the stranger good night, but before she could say a word, he launched his vicious attack, raining down blows on her head and face. With each blow, he let out a horrible grunt.

"Please stop," she begged as the first punch drove her to her knees. Immediately, she thought about the killer who was wanted by police for murdering two women. Lying at the side of the road, she was blinded by the shock of the attack and the blood that streamed from her head into her eyes.

The distant headlights of a car saved her. Her attacker picked her up and threw her over a low fence into a field, before running off. Staggering to her feet, she tried to walk, but she was disorientated and had no idea which way was home.

Covered in blood, she stumbled towards the road. A neighbour found her and brought her home. She fell through the door and into her mother's arms.

"What happened?" Janice cried, seeing the severe wound on her daughter's head. Janice rushed her to the hospital, where she stayed for two weeks.

"Why me?" Deirdre cried, when the nurses removed her bandages, and she saw the shocking extent of her injuries. Her eyes were black, and she had extensive bruising all over her body.

Initially, the investigators suspected that Deirdre had been attacked with a large stick. However, forensic analysis showed that a hammer was the most likely weapon.

George appealed for anyone who had been in the area on the night of the attack to come forward. He was confident that the attacker was a local man because of the lateness of the hour and the fact he knew Deirdre had a boyfriend. However, despite Deirdre's detailed description of her attacker, George was still no closer to solving the case.

Chapter 20

"Sir, there's been another murder," said the voice at the other end of the line in breathless desperation. The hair on the back of George's neck stood up. "A thirty-five year old woman has been found dead near Leeson Street."

"Who found her?" George asked.

"Her boyfriend found her at the edge of the park near their apartment block. She was charged with soliciting last year."

"I'm on my way." George's head was buzzing; this could be the case that confirmed they were dealing with a serial killer.

The aspen trees cast long shadows across the ground in an unexpected burst of late autumn sun that hung low in the cloudless sky. Lying on muddy ground in the shade of one of the trees and hidden from the road was a body. She lay on her side. Her face was turned towards the grass and concealed by her long, dark hair.

The moment he saw Melissa Levie, he knew she was the killer's third victim. There was the same vicious attack to the head as the other women and the same pattern of stab wounds and cuts to the body.

George brushed her hair to one side and saw the blood on her neck. Her eyes were glazed and staring. She wore a cream cardigan and a long suede skirt. There was a sock on her right foot, but the left foot was bare. Blood was matted in her hair and soiled her neck and cardigan. Leaves beside the body also had some blood spots, and a trail of blood ran from the body to a bag. The contents of the bag had spilled out onto the grass.

She wore a gold-plated watch on her left wrist. The glass was partly obscured by droplets of water inside. It was no longer working. The time had stopped at 11.50.

After her temperature was recorded and the body photographed, she was turned on her back on to a plastic sheet. There was a gaping wound at her throat, with soiling of the surrounding skin and the collar of her cardigan. A deep cut on her stomach had ripped through the lower abdominal wall.

George felt the ground shift beneath his feet. He stood with his head bowed and his hands shoved deep into his pockets, making fists. His knees ached from all the years of bending down, ducking under crime scene tape and too long spent squashing himself into spaces that weren't quite big enough for his broad shoulders and long legs.

Investigators were already conducting inquiries. Inquisitive neighbours stood in their doorways, wondering what was going on. Some invited the officers inside, but no one had heard or seen anything.

George rotated his head to ease the knots in his neck. His old rugby injury always played up in the cold weather. He looked at the victim in the short grass, trying to see her as someone's daughter, someone's friend, and not the depravity in front of him. How he longed to go home to his clean house, to take a shower and curl up under the freshly laundered duvet beside his wife.

He turned away from the enormity, aware of the coroner's officer standing behind him. Sharon tilted her head and studied his face, trying to read his mind. He stood there, without speaking.

"Anyone home?"

"Sorry."

"I thought I'd lost you there."

He let out a long, low sigh. "I've seen too much. I don't have much space left in my head for scenes like this."

Sharon patted his arm. "Shall we have a look inside?" she asked, leading the way.

George gathered his thoughts, took a breath, and held it for a moment. Then he followed her across the park and trudged up the concrete steps. The apartment block where Melissa had lived was shabby and squalid. An old mattress was propped against the wall in the corridor; someone had abandoned it there.

The one-bedroom apartment was in a shocking state, with no sign of any effort to clean the kitchen or bathroom. George's first thought was that the apartment had been used for one thing only: sex. The bedroom had a large double bed with a dressing table and heavy curtains closed across the small window.

The living area had a fake fireplace, which was plugged into the wall by a short cable. A pair of stiletto heels stood on the kitchen counter, beside a full ashtray and a bottle of cheap perfume. The threadbare carpet looked as if it hadn't been cleaned in years and the place stank of alcohol and stale cigarettes.

Shortly before midnight, forensics had completed their work. A thorough search of the apartment produced a diary among Melissa's meagre belongings. It contained the names of twenty men, most of whom were clients.

***

Melissa's boyfriend officially identified the body. Theirs was a strange, desultory relationship, made worse by the fact that she was a drug addict. The post-mortem continued until dawn. Sharon Tierney confirmed what they had seen in the other murders. There was a clear and established pattern: similar head injuries; similar arrangement of the clothing; and multiple stab wounds produced by several different instruments.

"I believe that the killer knocks his victims to the ground, making them immobile, by using the same hammer each time. Then he rearranges the clothes and inflicts the stab wounds with a different weapon, which provides the necessary satisfaction for him," Sharon concluded.

George's biggest fear was that the killer would strike again soon. He was convinced that there were people out there who had not come forward. He made several urgent appeals for witnesses before there was another murder, even asking local church and community leaders for assistance.

George organised a meeting with the city's psychiatrists in an unsuccessful attempt to get assistance from mental hospitals about patients who could be suspects.

Prostitutes were questioned in detail about their regular clients, even as they were also being cautioned for soliciting. On the one hand, the investigators needed the women's help; on the other, they wanted to put them out of business. Word went out from police, social workers and probation officers that women selling sex were in serious danger, especially those who stood alone in the dark, on street corners, trying to pick up men in cars.

A covert operation of static observations was mounted, with detectives recording the car registration numbers of drivers trying to pick up women in the red-light district. George felt that the killer was using his car to trawl Dublin for vulnerable women. He operated with deliberate stealth in choosing the women he wanted to kill. It was time to take offensive action rather than wait for the killer to strike again.

I Should Have Told You

Chapter 21

"Sir, you've got to read this!" The desk sergeant burst into the incident room, where George and Mike were pondering the timeline of the murders.

"Jesus Christ! There's no need to give me a heart attack." George stared at him and snatched the letter from his hands. "This better be good."

"It's from the killer."

George ripped open the letter and began to read.

" "DCI George Ellis,

"I am The Night Killer. You don't have any idea who I really am. Maybe I should tell you and put you out of your misery...or maybe not...The newspapers say I'm sick, but you say I'm clever. I'm not sick, I'm insane.

"I lie awake at night picturing my next kill. Maybe she will be the lovely brunette who works part-time at the cinema, and walks home alone down the dark laneway every Friday night at eleven. Maybe she will be the curvy blonde with the beguiling smile at my favourite pub. Either way, I'll cut them open and leave them naked for the whole world to see.

"Please stop making it so easy for me. Keep your mothers, wives, daughters and sisters off the streets, laneways, and parks.

"The first one was young and beautiful, but she's long dead. She's not the first, and she certainly won't be the last. She was quite the little fighter. It was fun. First, I cut the wire from the distributor. Then I waited while she dined alone in the restaurant. The battery was flat by the time she came out.

"I offered her my assistance. She was so willing to talk to me. I said my car was across the road, and that I'd be happy to give her a lift home. As we reached the outskirts of the village, I put my hand over her mouth and grabbed her by the neck, holding a knife to her throat.

"Her breasts were warm and firm under my hands, but I had only one thing on my mind. She squirmed and struggled as I choked her. I'll never forget the sound. Her lips twitched as she gasped for air. She let out a scream and I kicked her in the head to shut her up. I thrust the knife deep into her until it broke.

"I'm up to number six now, not three as the newspapers have written. You're only finding the easy ones; there will be a lot more soon. I'm getting quite annoyed with all the lies being told about me. In future, when I kill, I'll make them look like robberies gone wrong or murders of anger or maybe an accident. You won't have a clue and I won't be leaving any.

"I look like the photofit in the newspapers when I choose to look like that; the rest of the time I look completely different. I won't be telling you about my disguise. I'm a chameleon.

"I haven't left any fingerprints behind because I wear gloves every time I kill. I know I haven't left you much to work on. I enjoy torturing you.

"Doesn't it irritate you to have your nose rubbed in it? You're good, George, but I am better. You'll grow weary and then you'll leave me alone. I'll become another one of your cold cases that I see on the TV every night. I'm looking forward to the film about my life. I wonder who will play my part.

"I enjoy this game I'm playing. This letter should be published for the world to read. It might just save the next woman. If this letter isn't published, I will cruise around and kill off all the stray people or couples who are alone.

"School children make easy targets. Maybe I'll take down a school bus one of these afternoons. I'll shoot out the front tyre and then shoot the little brats as they come down the steps one by one.

"I feel the urge coming on again. I need help. I cannot reach out because this compulsion won't let me. It is impossible to control. Sometimes I feel like I'm drowning. Consider this a warning. I am coming for your girls.'"

"Do you think he's our man?" Mike asked.

"Who knows? It could be a hoax. Get forensics to have a look at it," George said, bagging the letter and handing it to Mike.

"Why did he address it to you?"

"Why not? Everyone knows I'm heading the investigation." George rubbed his tired eyes.

"Do you think he's lying about the number of victims?"

"I hope so," George sighed. "I really hope so."

"He's taunting us," Mike said. "He's trying to turn this into a contest between the hunter and the hunted, between the forces of good and evil. We have to find the bastard."

"The clock's ticking." George tugged at the skin around his thumb.

"When did you last sleep?" Mike asked.

"I don't know. I don't care. Terrible images keep spinning around in my head. If this man kills again, it will be my fault for not trying hard enough to catch him."

"I think you should go home, get some rest."

George stood up and stared out the window on the city below. "I can't go home with all this happening. I won't." He pinched the bridge of his nose and scowled. "I'm fine. Honestly."

He paced the floor, unable to sit still or stop thinking. His head was a city. He rubbed his forehead with the palm of his hand, trying not to think about the sights he'd witnessed during his twenty years of blood and marrow and bone.

He wandered the corridors of the building with its peeling plaster and smudged windows, observing the officers' tired faces under neon lights, glued to their flickering computer screens, and past the filing cabinets with their dreadful secrets.

He thought of the people out there in Dublin, the plain clothes and uniformed officers waiting and watching in chilly cars. Men and women who'd been up for two days straight and the others who had come in off sick leave and holidays.

He felt exhausted and worried about his wife and children sleeping at home alone. The letter had made the manhunt a personal affair between George and the killer.

Chapter 22

George had no idea what he was going to say at the press conference until he was sitting at the top of the room facing the journalists. Mike and their boss, Detective Chief Superintendent Eamonn Dwyer, flanked him: a silver-haired, handsome man with sharp blue eyes.

"These murders are a tragedy for the victims, their families, the police and for Ireland as a whole," George began. "We would like to ask the man who identifies himself as The Night Killer to please contact us." He paused, taking in the crowded room: the journalists, the cameramen, the flashing lights. "We know he's in turmoil emotionally and mentally. We can help him. We want to talk to him, so please call the number on screen.

"We would also like to appeal to the family of The Night Killer. His handwriting is being made available to the public on the news websites, on the police website, and on a Facebook tip page, which we've set up for this purpose.

"Somebody out there knows this man. He's a husband, a son, a brother, a friend, or a colleague. We're asking the public to look at the letter and see if you recognise the writing. Is he someone you know?

"Please remember that this man is in a great deal of pain. By helping us, you will be helping him. Once again, to the man calling himself The Night Killer, please contact us, for your own sake."

He looked into the crowd at the shifting cameras and their void compound eyes, and reeled off the telephone numbers again before getting to his feet. "No questions at this time. Thank you."

He gathered his papers and left the room, leaving the journalists clamouring for more. In the corridor, he leaned against the cool wall and closed his eyes, waiting for his heartbeat to slow and the anger and nausea to pass.

**

The killer bought *The Independent, The Examiner* and *The Times*, but not *The Herald*. He detested *The Herald*. Then he went to his favourite greasy spoon and ordered a full Irish breakfast. He shrugged off his coat and scarf and put them carefully on the back of his chair.

He added three heaped spoons of sugar to his tea, stirred it, and opened the first newspaper. His hands trembled in anticipation as he read the front-page headlines.

DUBLIN HOLDS IT'S BREATH... PRAYERS SAID AND VIGILS HELD FOR THE MURDERED WOMEN... HUNDREDS OF POLICE CANCEL LEAVE...DARK TIMES...

The killer glanced out the grubby window at the grey city as it came to life. He watched the market owners setting up their stalls of fruit and veg and fake designer clothes and handbags; the office workers hurrying to work with a coffee in one hand and a briefcase or a handbag in the other; and the college students ducking into the newsagents for a paper and a packet of cigarettes.

He turned back to the newspapers and to the photographs of his smiling victims. They weren't smiling anymore.

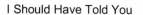

I Should Have Told You

Chapter 23

The killer is currently watching three women. In his safe, he keeps a key to each of their houses. He lets himself in and walks around when they're not home. He's learned how to be in a house and not be seen. He's been doing it for years.

The killer likes watching women on the street, in shops, on trains, and on buses. He falls in love with his victims long before he kills them. He's always careful to blend in. On winter evenings, he likes to wear a black wool coat over a business suit, a subtle tie, expensive glasses and a leather briefcase that contains his murder kit: a rope, a screwdriver, gloves and a hammer.

He likes to follow his prey home. Sometimes, it doesn't work out; they live in an apartment complex with security cameras at the entrance or he has a bad vibe, so he moves on to someone else. He always trusts his instincts.

He'll never forget his first victim. She was tall, porcelain-skinned and wore a mini skirt that made her endless legs seem even longer. She had long, red hair that fell in waves down her back and she was wearing ankle boots with no socks. Her pale, bare ankles in the hard lining of the boots gave him a powerful erotic charge.

She'd gotten off the bus a few stops from where he was staying. It was summer time and the smells of the city--traffic, hot tarmac and sweaty bodies--filled the air. She met her boyfriend outside a pub on the quay. He was tall, dark-haired, and muscular and carried himself with masculine assurance.

The killer hung back while the couple hugged outside the pub and kissed. He watched as their tongues slid over one another and nearly orgasmed when the man brushed the palm of his hand over her breast. He followed them home and watched them through the windows.

In the pitch-black darkness of the early morning hours, he broke in. It was a warm, sultry night in July and they'd forgotten to close the bathroom window. He climbed in and walked around the small, ground-floor apartment, watching them as they lay sleeping at opposite sides of the double bed. She slept on her back, naked, her auburn curls spread out across the pillow. He watched them from the open bedroom door, not worrying about being seen.

When he'd seen enough, he crawled across the bedroom floor and picked up her pink, lacy knickers. He sniffed them and stuffed them in his pocket.

Theirs was a summer romance. He was addicted to them. Their names were Angela and Douglas. Angela worked in sales, and Douglas was a lecturer.

The killer was on Angela's bus twice a week, enough for them to develop a nodding acquaintance. Several times, they were crammed against each other in the morning rush hour, holding the overhead rail, where he could smell her and feel the intensity of her secrets. She was perfect.

Douglas got over her death quickly. The killer followed him one evening to a bar and saw him meet another woman. He watched them drink too much, saw Douglas put his hand on her thigh, and kiss her across the table.

The killer still walks down Angela's street occasionally. He even pops into their local pub, but Douglas is long gone. He wonders what happened to him and if he found happiness with another woman. He feels a warm glow of nostalgia when he thinks about them together. They really were perfect.

Angela was his first kill. It had been wonderfully exhilarating, and the intense infatuation he had felt was like an illness. He'd learned how important it was to get over that heady feeling. He had to know his victim's moods and habits--good or bad.

***

Lilly Butler wants to be an actress. Her parents would prefer if she was anything else, but there were no "safe" career options anymore. Lilly's been taking acting lessons and there's a new confidence in her voice and the way she walks.

She emerges from the shabby doorway of the restaurant where she works part-time. She has a few words with another waitress before they say their goodbyes and part company. She huddles into her coat and starts walking.

Not far behind her, the killer watches and waits. He sees her wave goodbye and hurries along the dark street towards the alley. He's seen her take the shortcut through the alley many times before. It's only a five minute walk to where she lives.

She pauses for a moment and he holds his breath, willing her to keep walking. It doesn't really matter anyway; he's got a key, and he's already decided that tonight's the night. Lilly Butler: tall, blonde, beautiful, and absolutely lovely. He can't wait to get his hands on her.

Nervously, she glances over her shoulder, but doesn't see the man following in the shadows. She shivers and picks up her pace. Ever since the burglary the previous month, she's been edgy. The thought of someone in her room gives her the creeps. She thought her house keys had been stolen, but they'd turned up on her bedside table as if placed there by a ghost. She'd had a few crank calls recently--heavy breathers and hang ups--probably one of her little brother's creepy friends with a stupid crush.

Relieved, she sees the streetlights just up ahead. She hates taking the shortcut through the alley, but it takes twenty minutes off her walk. Almost home. She glances over her shoulder again.

A man is walking just behind her. She doesn't know him, but at once, she knows him completely. He races towards her. She draws in her breath, but before she can scream, he swings something at her head. She hears bone crack as he starts kicking her, and she falls to the ground.

No lights come on in the nearby houses. Nobody comes to the window. Nobody shouts or interferes. Nobody ever does.

Chapter 24

Early next morning, in the cold light of dawn, a woman on her way to work noticed a cowboy-style boot at the edge of the alley and a little further away what looked like a heap of clothes. She walked up the alley and realised that the heap of clothes was in fact the body of a young woman in her late teens.

Not long after the first responders arrived, Lilly's fourteen-year-old brother left their home to do his newspaper round. Walking past the alley, he saw several police officers and noticed that a body had been covered over. Then he recognised his sister's boot. She loved those boots.

Horrified, he ran home to tell his parents, who had assumed that Lilly was asleep upstairs having let herself in with her own key, as she usually did when she worked late. Finding her room empty, her distraught father called the police.

George was last to arrive at the scene. He flashed his badge at the log officer and ducked under the crime scene tape into glaring lights that threw the grey morning into high definition. No one looked like they'd slept for days.

Sharon Tierney nodded at him, but didn't say a word.

He shoved his fists into his pockets and thought of Gina, vaguely wondering what she was doing. The crime scene investigators were already there with their cameras, rulers and tape. The night air wasn't cold enough to eliminate the smell. He wanted to stand under a boiling shower and scrub his skin until it hurt.

He saw the pity in Sharon's eyes. News helicopters circled overhead, sweeping the streets with their searchlights.

The victim's body was covered by a blanket with the head visible at one end and the feet protruding at the other. A large plastic tent had been erected to protect the body from rain and onlookers. The area had been marked out with flagpoles, tapes and traffic cones, which showed where the victim had been dragged.

Sharon examined the body, noting the position of small stab wounds on the skin. The victim's face was streaked with blood. Two large wounds to her head were clearly visible, and blood had soiled the surrounding hair.

Footprints were visible in the mud nearby. Boots of a similar size had been found at the other crime scenes. A trail of boot prints was discovered going in the opposite direction from where the body had been dragged. The boot impressions showed that the wearer had run towards the nearby road and then slowed down.

The victim had multiple stab wounds to the front and back of the trunk, which had been caused by a sharply pointed object. She had fractures to the skull, consistent with being hit with a hammer, but more disturbingly there were injuries to the genitalia.

Examination of a mark on the victim's breast showed that a man with a crossbite in his upper front teeth had bitten her. Linda Keenan had had a similar mark on her breast.

George stepped away from the body, and ducked under the crime scene tape. Eyes watched him as he passed the officers, onlookers, and paramedics. At the edge of the scene, the blue and red lights of the squad cars flashed misery.

A scrum of faces had congregated already, eager to catch a glimpse. A news helicopter circled overhead. George buried his fists deep into his pockets and strode through the wet grass to a far corner of the park. He leaned against the wall, thick with wet ivy, and covered his face with his hands. The girl wasn't much older than his own daughter.

When he finished crying, Mike was standing beside him. George's eyes were red raw. He wiped his face with the back of his hand, mortified. Mike didn't say a word.

"Christ," George said eventually.

"I know."

Across the grass was the crime scene, the tape, the medical examiners and beyond them the park gates that led back into the city, the crowds, the cameras, the press, the mobile phones and the blaring radios on passing cars.

George scrubbed his face with his hands to rub some life back into it. He took a few deep breaths and set off across the park, while the universe churned beneath him.

***

Gina switched on the television to the newsreader as he pulled his serious face. "Another body has been found. Visibly upset police officers are at the scene."

She watched the footage as the helicopter camera zoomed in towards George stalking across the grass, away from the covered body, and followed him as he leaned against a wall, crying. Gina's hand went to her mouth. She switched off the television and immediately called him. His phone went straight to voicemail.

"Answer your bloody phone!" she yelled. He rarely answered his phone and it drove her crazy. She hung up and brushed her blonde fringe out of her eyes. She stared at the ceiling and repeated his name like a mantra: "George, George, George."

Gina didn't hear the keys in the lock or the door open. She didn't hear him walk down the hall and linger in the kitchen doorway, watching her.

"I'm home," he said, eventually.

She turned to look at him, ignoring the redundancy. "I called and left a message," she said. "Your phone was switched off, as usual."

"I'm sorry. Did you see the news?"

Her lower lip trembled with fury. "Of course I saw the bloody news! I've done nothing all day except talk about the news and worry about you. All of Ireland is talking about the news. The only one who hasn't talked to me about the bloody news is you!"

The intensity of her anger stunned him. He took a breath before responding. "Would you like some tea?"

"I can make my own tea, thanks," she snapped at him. She filled the kettle and leaned against the sink as it boiled, seething and glaring at him with fire in her eyes.

He sighed, exhausted. A muscle in his face twitched. "I should have called."

"I suppose you were too busy."

"I'm sorry," he said, taking off his coat and hanging it over a kitchen chair.

He moved towards her and pulled her into his arms. She sank into his embrace, and called him names under her breath as the fear left her. He rested his head on top of her hair, smelling the lemon-fresh scent of her. She could smell the sneaky cigarette he'd had earlier, but she didn't say anything. She pictured him pacing outside the station, guilt-ridden and worried.

"I should have called," he repeated.

She pulled away from him and started to make coffee. She stirred two spoons of sugar and a dash of milk into his cup, just the way he liked it, and handed him the cup.

"We need to talk," she said. "About us."

"What about us?"

"I think you know, George."

"Know what?"

"I hate this."

"What are you saying?"

"I hate what our marriage is becoming."

He felt weak. His hand shook as he put his cup on the table. "I don't understand."

"You do understand, George. How could you not? I've been saying the same thing for ages, louder and louder every time."

"Are you really going to do this today, seriously?" He rubbed a hand over his tired face.

"When would be a good time?"

"I don't know." He shrugged, all the fight gone out of him.

"I'm sick of trying to talk to you. You never listen to me. You just turn your back and walk away."

"I do listen."

"But you don't hear me."

"I don't understand you."

She laughed bitterly. "You're never here. You promise to make more of an effort, to come home early and spend more time with us, but you keep breaking your promises. I'm so tired of asking and begging. You keep telling me what I want to hear, but they're only words."

His heart sank. She felt sorry for him. "Don't say anything; it'll just be another broken promise."

He rubbed his temples and took a deep breath. "I'm sorry." He got up and splashed his face with cold water. Shaking, he sat back down in front of her and studied the early morning sunlight dancing against the kitchen wall.

"This is a mess," she said, eventually.

George sighed.

She got up and grabbed the car keys.

"Where are you going?"

"I don't know. I might go and see Dad."

She looked away and for a moment, he thought she was lying, but he didn't trust his judgement; he was angry, exhausted and bereft. Maybe he was imagining lies where there were none. He couldn't allow himself to go down that road. He watched her put her jacket and scarf on, and he knew that she wasn't going to her dad's or her friend's or anywhere else he knew.

More than anything, he wanted her to stay in their house with the yellow door and both their names on the deeds. He'd imagined growing old with her there. He'd die peacefully in his sleep, with Gina by his side.

He watched her zip up her jacket, standing there, waiting for him to say something--anything. "Please don't go." He hated the tremble in his voice.

"If I stay, we'll just argue."

"I'll go," he said, getting to his feet. He hoped she couldn't hear his desperation. "I'll go mad if I hang around the house all day, waiting for the phone to ring. You should stay, I'll go."

Immediately, he saw the disappointment in her eyes, and his stomach turned over. "Okay," she nodded slowly.

He picked up his coat and walked to the front door. "We'll get through this," he said, turning to her as she hovered in the hall. She was crying. He didn't know what to say. It had been too long since he'd said the right thing.

"Lock the door after me. Lock the windows too." He stepped outside and walked away, completely lost.

Joanne Clancy

Chapter 25

Gina took a long bath, ignoring the fact that she'd already showered twice that day. Then she lay on the couch in pyjamas and socks with her hair tied up on top of her head. The children were already fast asleep upstairs. She switched on the television and watched the news while she drank a bottle of red wine and grew teary. She checked her phone every few minutes. At midnight, she gave up checking and went to bed.

George opened the front door and trudged upstairs to the bedroom. Gina was already asleep, snoring softly. He didn't want to wake her, so he crept down the hall to the guest bedroom and slept in his clothes.

Around 4a.m., he cried out, loud enough to wake Gina. She padded to him in her bare feet and climbed into bed beside him. Neither of them could sleep, so they flicked through the channels on the television at the foot of the bed.

It happened in an instant. One minute they were watching a true crime programme, and the next minute their lives had changed forever. It was a special on two unsolved murder cases from the 1970s. The killer had struck terror into the women of Dublin and had never been caught.

Gina and George were transfixed. Neither of them could take their eyes off the image on the screen.

"It's you," Gina whispered, fear clutching her heart.

"It's not me," George said. He went to the study and picked up the photo on his desk. They looked from the photo to the television and back. It was as if someone had taken a photo of George and placed it on a "Wanted" poster. He knew immediately who the killer was.

"It's my father."

***

The sequel to *I Should Have Told You* will be available in February 2015. Sign up to the newsletter **at JoanneClancy.com to receive an email when the sequel is released.**

If you enjoyed *I Should Have Told You*, there are three more books in the series: ***Traceless, If You Tell Anyone, The Detective's Wife* and *The Gift*.** Although the books are part of a series, they can also be read as standalone novels, and are available to buy exclusively at Amazon or free with Kindle Unlimited.

Traceless

By

Joanne Clancy

TRACELESS. Some people should never be found...

Adam Stoltz vanishes in the middle of the night.

His girlfriend, Darcey Ackerman, is the last person to see him alive.

Left for dead, and with nowhere to turn, Darcey quickly learns the true meaning of love and loss.

She becomes obsessed with finding out what really happened to Adam, but is drawn into a deadly game of cat and mouse, where she's already several moves behind.

Someone is watching her, and she's about to discover that there's a fine line between love and hate...

REVIEWS:

If you like authors such as Gillian Flynn or Rachel Abbott then this is definitely a novel for you. This is a super fast paced thriller that keeps you guessing right to the end.

Although it is nominally a missing persons book, it actually turns more into a psychological thriller as the investigators try to unravel what really happened.

The ending was definitely a surprise, you will never guess it. It marks the book out from others in the genre. John Forrester, The Crime Scene

I loved this book. If I had an award to hand out for "best hook in a novel," Clancy would win the gold medal. The minute I started reading my eyeballs nearly popped out of my head. Traceless keeps the action moving along at a nice pace and crosses the finish line with the momentum of an Olympic sprinter. Belinda, Every Free Chance Book Reviews

If you like fast-paced, edge of your seat psychological thrillers that are impossible to put down, you'll love Traceless.

*** Best seller in Crime Fiction, Kidnapping, and Mystery, Thriller & Suspense ***

If You Tell Anyone

By

Joanne Clancy

Love, lies, and a deadly secret...how well can two people ever really know each other?

Victoria Spencer is in love with the perfect man, until she discovers his deadly secret. Digging deep into Jason Ford's past, she discovers the devastating truth of his private world--a world he has tried to keep hidden from her.

Jason is desperately trying to balance his two lives, but he is running out of time...killing time, and when a woman turns up dead, the finger of suspicion points squarely at him.

However, Detective George Ellis gets the feeling that there's more to the murder than meets the eye. His investigation leads him to probe the dark heart of evil, as he unwittingly helps Victoria in her pursuit of justice.

Victoria has learned to mistrust everyone around her. She will do anything to protect herself, but what if it's not enough?

Joanne Clancy

REVIEWS
If you like fast-paced thrillers, you'll love this book! Izzy, Amazon customer

I never imagined the ending. This is a must read book. Tracy Jillard

One hell of a mystery. Ashley, Amazon customer

Best seller in International Mystery & Crime

The Detective's Wife

By

Joanne Clancy

Life can change in an instant.

What if your life was one big lie? What if someone was about to discover your darkest secret?

Ben Miller is torn between two worlds. He has spent a lifetime running from the secrets and lies of his past, until an unexpected encounter forces him to face the consequences of what he did one fateful night seven years ago.

Vanessa Murphy is a high-powered lawyer, used to getting her own way--whatever the cost. However, the pretence of living a successful life is about to come crashing down around her. Soon, she will be locked away and hated, unless she can get rid of Ben Miller, who is the only piece of damning evidence against her.

What happens when the past and present lives of two strangers horribly collide?

Find out in The Detective's Wife, a story about the secrets we keep, the ties that bind us, and the true cost of the lies we tell.

Best seller in Crime Fiction> Kidnapping

The Gift

By

Joanne Clancy

Julie wants only one gift this holiday season, but it's going to take a Christmas miracle to make her wish come true.

Julie Hamilton loves Christmas. It's her favorite time of year, from the cinnamon smell of freshly baked mince-pies to the excitement of buying gifts for family and friends, decorating the tree, and hanging stockings for Santa Claus on the mantelpiece.

This Christmas promises to be extra special because she's expecting the perfect gift--her first baby--on Christmas Eve.

However, a chance encounter turns her world upside down, and soon, she's praying for her very own Christmas miracle.

Can the spirit of the Christmas season and the kindness of strangers find a way to make her wish come true?

Praise for Joanne Clancy
I love this author's unique way of
storytelling.Robin Lee, Amazon Top 500 Reviewer

I thoroughly enjoyed this read which was at
times Christmassy and festive and then tense and
dramatic. Highly recommended. Elaine G., Amazon
Top 50 Reviewer

A sign of a gifted author is the ability to
transport her readers, place them right in the middle
of the storyline and allow them to feel the range of
emotions that the characters in the book are going
through. Joanne Clancy is that type of author. ~Erin
Brady

Joanne Clancy draws you in from the first
sentence and doesn't let go! She has a way with
words that keeps you begging for more! Having read
previous works by this author, I know there is a great
deal of suspense, heartache, joy, and a virtual
maelstrom of emotions in my future! ~ Deb. A,
Amazon Customer

The Offering

By

Joanne Clancy

It was the beginning of everything and also the end...

The full moon crept across the sky, spilling light on to the gaps between the trees. The search party pushed their way deeper into the forest. The light from their torches showed them the way.

Laura Kildare walked in a dream-like state, past the barriers and the groups of police officers. The forest was full of strange faces, searching in the wrong direction, oblivious to where Sofia and Ben lay.

Laura sensed something in the moment before she saw it. A sudden shot of adrenaline pumped through her blood. Something caught her eye as she pushed her way through the dense undergrowth; it was Sofia's gold necklace.

Then she saw Sofia's body. The rust-coloured pine needles had fallen on her like decoration. Laura screamed; her face was the colour of a ghost. It was a gruesome canvas that would haunt her. There was no sign of Ben.

Sofia Sheridan was a French musician who moved to the remotest part of Ireland to forget her past and start again. It was the beginning of everything and also the end...

A Daughter's Secret

By

Joanne Clancy

Two can keep a secret, if one of them is dead...

Millionaire businessman, Brent Ford, has a past that he has spent twenty years trying to erase. However, someone is lurking in the shadows, unwilling to forgive and forget.

The seed of his murder was planted decades ago, and the killer has been on a one-way course to disaster ever since.

Only two people know the truth behind the deadly secret, but they have promised not to tell...

5 Star Review from Amazon Top 500
Reviewer
This murder/mystery was excellent. Every
time Joanne Clancy writes another crime story she
changes it up. This time you don't know who the
killer is, but you get to watch. You definitely have
many motives, no hard evidence, except a key that
unlocked the door for the murderer and the shocking,
twisted ending...It left me absolutely speechless....
~ Robin Lee, Amazon Top 500 Reviewer

5 Star Review from Amazon Top 1000
Reviewer
The plot was amazing and had its share of
heart stopping drama. I loved the characters and am a
great fan of Joanne Clancy. It's as if I can't get enough
of her. This was a wonderful story. It had all the
deceit and drama that one could pack into a story, and
the polished writing continued through the entire
work. I would definitely recommend this book to
anyone.
~ Mary Ann, Amazon Top 1000 Reviewer

Killer Friends

By

Joanne Clancy

Keep your friends close, but your enemies closer...

Flashes from the forensic cameras made lightning strikes against the darkness.

Detective Emma Cole screeched to a halt in front of the yellow police tape. Strands of the crime scene ribbon fluttered in the biting wind, while the lights from the police squad cars pulsated a warning that something terrible had happened.

At first glance, it seemed that the friends had been partying too much, but the blood told the real story.

Detective Emma Cole walked upstairs. She paused briefly outside the first bedroom before opening the door. Cautiously, she took a step inside and stopped abruptly. Nothing could have prepared her for the sight that met her eyes...

Joanne Clancy

Watched

By

Joanne Clancy

Darkness turned to light as the full moon lost its potency. The cold light of dawn crept over the horizon as the three-second flash from the lighthouse dimmed. The valley was still and quiet in the frosty morning air.

It was shortly after half past nine when Anna Roche drove carefully past the neighbouring house, wary of the black ice on the road, around the sharp bend, and down the steep, bumpy laneway.

Something caught her eye as she neared the bottom of the lane. A piece of red material fluttered in the wind, stuck on the low, barbed-wired fence at the edge of the field. Then she saw the body, huddled at the base of the fence. She slammed her foot on the brake. Her heart was pounding as she opened the driver's door and got out. There was blood, a lot of blood, pooled around the body. She screamed and ran as fast as she could for help.

The bloody, lifeless body was that of Alexandra Kingston, an artist of international acclaim. Alexandra was a regular visitor to Hook Head, the sleepy fishing village in County Wexford, Ireland. She loved the wild remoteness of the place, where she went to escape her hectic lifestyle, and spend some much-coveted time alone.

She told her fiancé she would be leaving Hook Head the following day, December 31, just in time to welcome in the New Year with him in London, but she never made it home…

Kindle best seller in International Mystery & Crime

Killing Time

By

Joanne Clancy

Everyone makes choices, but choices have consequences – consequences that may cost Jack Martin his life. Jack is forced to deal with the past, while desperately trying to balance the present, but he is running out of time...killing time.

Eric Martin is murdered in cold blood, while his wife lies sleeping beside him. She is savagely beaten and left for dead. Somehow, she survives the brutal attack. A two million euro inheritance seems to be the motive for the murder, and the finger of suspicion points squarely at Jack.

However, Detective Chief Inspector Charlie Scott gets the feeling that there's more to the crime than money. Her investigation leads her to probe the dark heart of the Martin family, where she uncovers the horrifying story that is at once a bloody murder mystery and a heart-breaking story of the worst kind of betrayal.

Joanne Clancy

Best seller in International Mystery & Crime

I Should Have Told You

Made in the USA
San Bernardino, CA
30 July 2015